T. Rex needs specs

Lesley Sims

Illustrated by David Semple

Deep in Dino Forest,
T. Rex is out exploring...

He falls **CRASH!** down a massive hole.

He hobbles home, but on the way
he stumbles on a stump.

He bashes into tree trunks...

and falls over with a **BUMP!**

The next day, he goes out
and sees his friend, Triceratops.

"Hello! How ARE you?" T. Rex cries.
"I'm heading to the shops."

T. Rex turns red. "Let me explain..."

You thought the tree was ME?

"T. Rex, you need some specs!" she says.
"You can't go on this way."

He blinks and nods.

EYE SPY SPECS

"I think you're right.
I'll buy a pair today!"

Ankylosaurus sits him down.

"Which letters can you see?"

"Letters?" T. Rex asks. He frowns.

"It's all a blur to me."

Ankylosaurus checks his specs.
"Yes, here's a pair for you!"

T. Rex grins and puts them on...
then gives a mighty roar.

HELP! A monster!
Quick, all run!

He dashes for the door.

Ankylosaurus calls, "Come back!
Have you not seen yourself before?"

He holds the mirror up and smiles.

That was YOUR face, T. Rex!

"Perhaps you need more friendly frames.
I have a range of specs."

Now T. Rex can see everything.
He doesn't trip or fall.

And as for which new specs he chose...

...well, he took them all!

Starting to read

Even before children start to recognize words, they can learn about the pleasures of reading. Encouraging a love of stories and a joy in language is the best place to start.

About phonics

When children learn to read in school, they are often taught to recognize words through phonics. This teaches them to identify the sounds of letters that are then put together to make words. An important first step is for children to hear rhymes, which help them to listen out for the sounds in words.

You can find out more about phonics on the Usborne website at **usborne.com/Phonics**

Phonics Readers

These rhyming books provide the perfect combination of fun and phonics. They are lively and entertaining with great storylines and quirky illustrations. They have the added bonus of focusing on certain sounds so in this story your child will soon identify the *x* sound, as in **exploring** and **explain.** Look out, too, for rhymes such as **triceratops** – **shops** and **tree** – **me**.

Reading with your child

If your child is reading a story to you, don't rush to correct mistakes, but be ready to prompt or guide if needed. Above all, give plenty of praise and encouragement.

Edited by Jenny Tyler
Designed by Sam Whibley

Reading consultants: Alison Kelly and Anne Washtell

First published in 2023 by Usborne Publishing Limited, 83-85 Saffron Hill, London EC1N 8RT, United Kingdom.
usborne.com Copyright © 2023 Usborne Publishing Limited. The name Usborne and the Balloon logo are registered
trade marks of Usborne Publishing Limited. All rights reserved. No part of this publication may be reproduced,
stored in a retrieval system or transmitted in any form or by any means without prior permission of the publisher.
First published in America 2023. UE.